MRS. WATSON
WANTS YOUR TEETH

STORY BY

Alison McGhee

PICTURES BY

Harry Bliss

SCHOLASTIC INC.

New York Toronto London Auckland Sydney
Mexico City New Delhi Hong Kong Buenos Aires

ISBN-13: 978-0-545-03011-3
ISBN-10: 0-545-03011-0

12 11 10 9 8 7 6 5 4 3 2 1   7 8 9 10/0

Printed in the U.S.A.   40

This edition first printing, March 2007

The pictures in this book were done in black ink and watercolor on Arches 90 lb. watercolor paper.

The display lettering was created by Jane Dill.

The text type was hand-lettered by Paul Colin.

Designed by Suzanne Fridley and Scott Piehl

For Min O'Brien
—A. M.

For my hilarious, toothless,
hockey-playing son, Alex
—H. B.

I have a secret. . . .

First grade begins today, and I'm in BIG trouble.

It's a known fact that Mrs. Watson, the first-grade teacher, is a three-hundred-year-old alien who steals baby teeth from her students.

How do I know? A second grader told me.

My secret? I have a loose tooth! It's my first one.

It's so loose that every time I take a bite, I expect it to fall right out.

I miss my kindergarten teacher. She was the one who taught me how to tie my shoes.

I did it!

She let me bring stuffed animals to class.

And she did *not* have a "treat box" or a purple tongue.

PINK

MRS. WATSON'S
LOST TOOTH
GALLERY
1990 —
WHO
WILL
IT BE
THIS YEAR
?!
MRS.
WATSON
L.A.
NEW
YORK
TEXAS

AFTER SHARING...

I want to get a good look at Mrs. Watson's purple tongue . . .

and those
earrings . . .

and her "pearl"
necklace. . . .

At snack time, I look up. Guess who is right there?

It's going to be a long year—a long, silent, snackless, tooth-protecting year.

At recess, I look up. Guess who's right there?

BACK IN CLASS...

Does that boy know that Mrs. Watson is really a three-hundred-year-old alien with a purple tongue who needs earthling baby teeth in order to survive? I have to warn him!

Mrs. Watson comes toward *me* with the treat box!

And that's when it happens. . . .

I get a good look at Mrs. Watson's pearl necklace...

and her earrings...

and I get an extra good look at the treat box!

AFTER SCHOOL...